Doctor Ted

by Andrea Beaty and Pascal Lemaitre

SIMON AND SCHUSTER
LONDON   NEW YORK   SYDNEY

For Michael, my love
AB

To Doctor Caude Haber
PL

SIMON AND SCHUSTER
First published in Great Britain in 2008
by Simon & Schuster UK Ltd
Africa House, 64-78 Kingsway,
London WC2B 6AH
A CBS COMPANY

Originally published in 2008 by
Margaret K. McElderry Books, New York

Text copyright © 2008 Andrea Beaty
Illustrations copyright © 2008 Pascal Lemaitre

A CIP catalogue record for this book is available
from the British Library upon request

ISBN: 978 1 84738 319 8

Printed in China
1 2 3 4 5 6 7 8 9 10

One morning
Ted woke up,
got out of bed, and
bumped his knee.

"That's not good," thought Ted.
"I need a doctor."

He looked everywhere,

but he couldn't find one.

And since Ted couldn't find a doctor . . .

. . . he became a doctor.

Doctor Ted didn't have an office,
so he made one.

Doctor Ted didn't have a big bandage,
so he made one of those too.

"Now all I need is a patient,"
he thought.

So he waited for one to arrive.

He waited . . .

and he waited . . .

and he waited.

"Nice waiting room," thought Doctor Ted.

Then he waited some more.

"I think it's time for a house call," he thought.

"Hello?" he called.

Doctor Ted's mother was in the kitchen.

"You have measles," said Doctor Ted.
"We should operate."

"Those are my freckles,"
said his mother.
"Come on, it's time
for breakfast."

At school Doctor Ted sat in the third row of Mrs Johnson's class. All around him, children coughed and sniffled and sneezed.

Doctor Ted smiled.
"Patients," he thought.

The patients were very germy.

At lunchtime Doctor Ted took their temperatures and their blood pressure.

He gave them good medical advice, and they were very grateful.

Doctor Ted was such a good doctor that
even Mrs Johnson came to see him!

"You can't be a doctor
in the canteen!" she said.

"You have mumps,"
said Doctor Ted.
"Crutches could help."

"Those are my cheeks," said Mrs Johnson.
"Come on, it's time for lunch."

Headteacher Bigham walked in.

Doctor Ted could tell
he was very sick.
He needed a doctor.

"We already have a school doctor who
visits on Fridays," said Headteacher
Bigham with a smile.

"You have gingivitis," said Doctor Ted. "You need a full-body cast."

Headteacher Bigham frowned.

"You also have bad breath," said Doctor Ted.
"You need an injection."

The headteacher's face turned bright red.

"And a fever!" said Doctor Ted. "You need a transplant."

"WE ALREADY HAVE A SCHOOL DOCTOR!"

Headteacher Bigham pointed towards the door.

"We could do something about those smelly feet," said Doctor Ted.

"Go home!" said Headteacher Bigham.

Doctor Ted was very sad.
He packed up his big bandage and went home.

That night he took two biscuits and went straight to bed.

The next day at breaktime,
Ted sat on a bench and sighed.

He watched Frances Sylvester do
gymnastics on the monkey bars.
She was very talented.

Everyone thought so, especially Mrs Johnson
and Headteacher Bigham.

Frances finished her routine with a triple twisting somersault.

She landed on Mrs Johnson.

"OUCH!" cried Mrs Johnson.
"My ankle!"

Headteacher Bigham ran this way and that.

"HELP!" he yelled.
"Call an ambulance!
Call the fire brigade!
Call the library!
JUST CALL SOMEBODY!"

But Doctor Ted was already there.

He wrapped Mrs Johnson's ankle with his big bandage. He checked her vision and her tonsils.

"Take two biscuits," he said.
"You'll feel better in the morning."

Just then, the ambulance arrived.
And the fire brigade.
And the librarians.

"It's a good thing
you had Doctor
Ted," they all said.

"There's always room for another
school doctor," said Mrs Johnson.

"My work here is done," said Doctor Ted. "Keep the bandage."

Headteacher Bigham's face turned bright red. "You really should do something about that fever," said Doctor Ted.

That night Doctor Ted closed his office, packed away his stethoscope . . .

and went to sleep,
knowing he had
done a good job.

The next morning Ted woke up, got out of bed, and sniffed the air. It smelled like burnt toast.

"That's not good," thought Ted.
"I need a fire engine . . ."